ALBERT

ALBERT

by

ALISON JEZARD

Illustrated by

MARGARET GORDON

LONDON
VICTOR GOLLANCZ LTD
1970

575 00100 3

First published October 1968
Second impression May 1970

Printed in Great Britain by
The Camelot Press Ltd., London and Southampton

For my daughter Hilary
who introduced me to Albert

CONTENTS

I

ALBERT MEETS HENRY

Albert pushed his black-and-white checked cap to the back of his head, scratched his left ear with his paw, and gazed at the empty step. That was just the trouble, the step shouldn't have been empty.

There were eight stone steps altogether, and they led from the area outside Albert's door up to the street level of 14 Spoonbasher's Row. Usually, of course, the steps were empty, unless someone was going up to the street, or coming down to Albert's door, but on this bright, sunny April morning, Albert had decided to spring-clean his basement bed-sitting room and had been carrying out rugs and chairs and his geranium. Only a few minutes earlier, Albert had carried his umbrella stand outside and placed it carefully on the third step, where he could get at it to wash it down. Coming back with a pail of soapy water, he found the step empty.

Albert put down the pail, straightened his cap and climbed the eight steps to the street. Looking both ways up and down Spoonbasher's Row he could see at first no sign of his umbrella stand, and then he noticed a horse and cart, about twenty yards up the road. On the cart was a pile of all sorts of oddments such as mattresses, chairs, plant pots and fenders and, perched on top of the heap of junk, was Albert's umbrella stand.

Full of indignation, Albert went over and stood in front of the horse.

"What," demanded Albert, "is my umbrella stand doing on your cart?"

"Pardon?" said the horse.

"My umbrella stand."

"I never carry an umbrella myself," remarked the horse.

"Neither do I," replied Albert, "but I like to have a stand for my friends to put theirs in."

"Then why did you put it out as junk?" asked the horse.

"I didn't. I was going to wash it down and when I turned my back for two minutes it had gone from the step."

The horse slowly turned his head and surveyed the contents of the cart.

"I can't see an umbrella stand," he said.

"That's it, right on top."

"Do you mean that thing like a piece of green china drainpipe with knobbly flowers round it?"

"That's it."

"And do you mean to say you want it back?" asked the horse in a surprised voice.

"That umbrella stand," explained Albert slowly and distinctly, "belonged to my grandmother. I have my grandfather's marble clock on the mantelpiece, too," he added proudly.

"Could you lift it down?"

"No, I'm afraid I can't reach."

"Well," said the horse, "my master is not the easiest person to get along with and he might take exception to your wanting it back, after putting it out on the step, but," he went on, ignoring Albert's growl, "if you came round to the junk-yard this evening after seven he will be out and you could take it home again . . . if you really want to," he added, with another glance at Albert's grandmother's umbrella stand.

"Yes, I do really want to. It is a very fine umbrella stand."

"The yard is in Candle Lane, the big green gates,"

the horse went on. "Come just after seven and I can open the latch of the little door in the gates for you. My name is Henry," he added.

"I'm Albert." The checked cap was raised politely. "Thank you very much. I will see you this evening and now I had better get back in case anything happens to my geranium. You will try not to go over any bumps, won't you? That pile doesn't look very safe to me," Albert added anxiously.

"I'll be careful," promised Henry, and Albert returned to the job of cleaning out his house.

By tea-time, the little basement room was shining with polish, and a bright fire burned in the grate. The red geranium stood on the newly washed window-sill, the patch-work bedspread had been freshly laundered, and grandfather's marble clock had been given a very special dusting. It all looked very cosy and comfortable. On the hearth stood the brown china teapot full of fresh tea, and in a frying-pan on the gas ring which stood on a table near the fireplace two fat sausages were sizzling away and giving off a very interesting smell.

Albert, his paws well scrubbed and his checked cap thoroughly brushed, sat in his basket chair holding a slice of bread to the flames on the prongs of a toasting fork. When the bread was golden brown on both sides, Albert spread it carefully with butter while it was still hot, tipped the sausages out on to a plate and sat down to his meal at the table which he had spread with a clean, white cloth.

After he had finished his tea and washed up the dishes, Albert sat down in his favourite basket chair and put his paws on the fender. He had time for half an hour's rest before going round to the junk-yard and he was quite weary but very pleased with himself as he looked round

his comfortable bed-sitting room. Through the window he could look up to the street and watch legs going by on the pavement above his area, and, as he watched, the street lamp just outside went on to light the way for them.

Soon the marble clock told Albert to set off for Candle

Lane and he reached the door in the big, green gate just as Henry clicked up the latch for him.

"Hello," said Henry, and Albert asked anxiously, "Is it here?"

"Yes, quite safe," Henry told him and added, "I have found something I think you would like to have. It would make up for all your trouble."

Henry led the way over the cobbled yard to a big open shed and there stood the umbrella stand, but there was something in it.

"What is it?" asked Albert.

"Actually," explained Henry, "it's an umbrella."

Albert lifted the umbrella carefully out of the stand and examined it. It was very large and very black with a wooden handle carved to look like a dog's head.

"Do you like it?" asked Henry.

Albert was most impressed. "It's magnificent," he said. He put it back in the stand. "It looks quite at home there, doesn't it?" he went on. "I mean as if it belonged there?"

"I rather like it," agreed Henry. "Will you be able to carry both of them?"

"Oh yes, and thank you very much for the umbrella and for looking after my stand."

"That's all right," Henry replied, "and you'll be more careful where you put your junk next time, won't you?"

Albert took a deep breath and started to explain once more about his grandmother's umbrella stand but, instead, he picked it up with the big, black umbrella in it and carried it to the gate.

"Goodnight, Albert," said Henry. "Come and see me again one evening and I will show you round."

"Thank you," Albert called back. "Goodnight, Henry."

Very carefully Albert carried his burden along the lanes towards home. On the corner of Spoonbasher's Row a policeman was standing.

"Hello, Albert," he called. "What are you doing?"

"I'm taking my umbrella stand home," Albert told him.

"It's coming on to rain quite heavily," remarked the policemen.

"Yes, I noticed that," answered Albert politely. "I hope you won't get very wet, Mr Green. Goodnight."

"Goodnight, Albert."

Police Constable Green stood on the corner in his dark cape and tall helmet and watched Albert carrying his umbrella stand, with the rolled umbrella in it, along the street to his home while the rain poured steadily down.

II

ALBERT FILLS A SPACE

It was one Tuesday dinner-time when Albert decided to buy a picture.

Every Tuesday, at one o'clock, Albert took a little white basin and a napkin from the cupboard and went along the street to old Mrs Rose's shop on the corner of Spoonbasher's Row and Pudding Lane.

Albert loved the small London lanes, many of which were still named after the trades which, in old London, were all carried out in the same streets. Albert's own street was named after the men who used to entertain the theatre queues by singing some old music-hall song and accompanying themselves by rattling two spoons together like castanets. Albert had tried it himself once at a party, but he found it difficult to hold two spoons in one paw. There had been one man with a piano accordion, and two spoonbashers, and Albert had found that he could make a very good background noise by sliding his paw up and down an old washing board.

Mrs Rose was a plump, elderly lady and her little shop was full of good smells from cooked meats. Black puddings, white puddings, sausages and, on Tuesdays, faggots with peas. Mrs Rose would put two faggots and a big spoonful of peas into the little basin, cover it with the cloth, and Albert would hurry home to eat it while it was still hot.

On this particular Tuesday, he was just chewing the last crunchy brown mouthful when he noticed the space on the wall over Grandfather's marble clock.

It wasn't any more spacious than usual, in fact it had always been there, with a small damp patch shaped like a butterfly, which always reappeared however carefully Albert distempered the wall apple green. Something to hang in the space—and the answer seemed to be a picture, but a picture of what?

Albert looked all round his cosy room from the green door with two glass panels and a dark red curtain to draw across it when it was cold, past the two pegs on the wall, on one of which hung his best Sunday cap, and on to the bed. He was very proud of his bed. A good iron bed with four brightly polished knobs, one on each post, and a very gay patchwork cover.

Near the bed was a cupboard where Albert kept his clean sheets and towels, cups, saucers, plates and his frying-pan. Behind a screen was the sink and a back door to the yard. Under the sink was a smaller cupboard where Albert kept his food.

In the middle of the room there was a small round table covered with a red cloth which had bobbles all round the edge and had belonged to his mother. There was a wooden chair at the table where he was sitting, and a cosy basket chair on the hearth-rug in front of the fire. On the window sill was his bright red geranium.

Albert was no nearer deciding what kind of picture was needed, so he told himself he would see what he could find and, taking his brown leather purse from behind the clock, he set off for the market in Petticoat Lane, which was only a few minutes' walk away.

All along the street there were stalls set up selling all sorts of exciting and interesting things and many of the

stall-holders knew Albert and called a cheery greeting to him. He waved his paw and grinned back at them, but didn't stop till he got to Mrs Arbuthnot's flower stall. He always stopped there and sniffed at the great bunches of daffodils, jonquils, narcissus, and tulips. He poked his nose into a bowl of violets and Mrs Arbuthnot said, "Hello, Albert, how are you today?"

"Very well, thank you, Mrs Arbuthnot." Albert touched his cap politely. "I hope you don't mind me sniffing your flowers."

"Bless you, no luv, you sniff away. I don't expect you'll sniff all the smell away." And she threw back her head and laughed out loud. Then she said, "Here you are, Albert, here are a few violets left over, they'll cheer you up and make you think of spring."

Albert thanked her very much and, carrying his little bunch of violets, he moved on to where a man was auctioning watches.

"I'm not going to ask you for one pound, ladies and gentlemen. I'm not going to ask you for ten shillings for this magnificent watch," and he held up a large watch by its leather strap and gave it an admiring look. "For this superb watch with all moving parts and real genuine rubies, I am only asking seven-and-six. Three half dollars and it's yours, sir," he called to Albert.

"No, thank you," called Albert, "I have my grandfather's marble clock," and he went on to the stall he had meant to visit.

He often stood in front of Mr Brown's stall and gazed at the fascinating objects for sale. Today there was a silver-plated cake dish, a big blue ornamental flowerpot, a china jug with roses on it and a bust of a man with a pointed beard and a chip out of his left ear. At one end of the stall there was a pile of second-hand books.

"I really must buy myself a book one day," Albert told himself, "it would look rather nice lying on the table beside the lamp."

Mr Brown turned round from his last customer and

said, "Good morning, Albert, you look as though you want to buy something today."

"Yes, I want to fill up a space."

"Well, here's just the thing." Mr Brown brought forward a tall stand which looked to Albert like a wooden palm tree without leaves.

"Fill a lovely space, this would," advised Mr Brown.

"What is it?" asked Albert.

"It's an 'atstand. A lovely me'ogany 'atstand."

"It isn't that kind of a space," Albert told him. "It's on a wall."

"On a wall! I've got just the thing." Mr Brown brought out from behind the stall a round flat object with a brass lid and a long handle.

"I already have a frying-pan," Albert objected.

"Frying pan! It's a warming-pan. You put hot coals in it and shove it in the bed. Why, this may be the very warming pan that warmed the feet of the great Queen Elizabeth I of England for all you know. All the best people have warming pans on their walls these days."

"I was thinking of a picture," said Albert. "I haven't got room for a hatstand and I already have a hook for my Sunday cap and I don't think a warming-pan would look quite right, although it is a beautiful warming-pan," he added hastily, "but I think perhaps a picture."

"Well now, a picture," Mr Brown rummaged about. "How about this portrait of an old lady. A dear old white-haired lady. Might be your grandmother."

"She could hardly be my grandmother," replied Albert a little stiffly.

"No, I suppose not. Well, let's see. How about this one of a woodland scene, all trees and autumn leaves. Make you feel at 'ome, that would."

"I'm not that kind of a bear," Albert reminded him gently, trying not to be too unhelpful, and then he saw it. His picture. It was about 18 inches by 12 inches and it was leaning against a box behind the stall in a narrow gold frame.

"That one, please," said Albert pointing his paw.

"That one?" asked Mr Brown surprised. He picked it up and gave the glass a dust over with his sleeve. "Lovely picture that is," he agreed. "Nearly hung it on me own wall."

He held it up at arm's length. Against a background of dark, windswept clouds on a raging, white-crested sea, a three-masted ship in full sail was beating against the wind straight out of the picture; pennants streaming and bow-wave foaming pure white against the dark oak hull.

Albert was entranced. He could feel himself already master of this gallant ship, shouting orders to his men in the teeth of the gale with the spray lashing his face. He came back to earth with a bump when Mr Brown said,

"Well, seeing it's you, Albert, fifteen bob."

"Seeing it's me, Mr Brown, could you make it twelve-and six?"

"All right," laughed Mr Brown, and Albert quickly took out a ten shilling note and a half-crown and paid it over before the other could change his mind. A few minutes later he was on his way home carrying the picture very carefully under one arm and his purse and violets in the other paw.

At the end of Petticoat Lane, he paused and sniffed. Hot chestnuts! There they were popping and sizzling away over the brazier and smelling delicious. Once more Albert set off for home and now he had added a paper bag to his collection. Soon he was carrying everything carefully down the area steps to his front door and

in a very short time he had found a hammer and a nail, and his picture was hung. It looked just right and seemed to be the perfect partner for the marble clock.

Albert put the violets into an egg-cup and stood it in the middle of the table-cloth. He took a big sniff at them and then he sat down in his basket chair, put his feet on the fender, opened his bag of chestnuts, and gazed at his beautiful picture, and as he slowly chewed the hot fragrant nuts, he was back in command on the bridge of his sailing ship.

III

ALBERT IS PUMPED OUT

Albert was on the quarter-deck of his ship. With his admiral's cap squarely on his head, he was directing the battle of his small squadron of gallant ships against terrible odds.

"Fire!" shouted Albert, and as the guns roared out, the thunder rolled and echoed round Spoonbasher's Row and Albert woke up with a start and opened his eyes. Then he closed them again because he was obviously still dreaming. When he found that he wasn't dreaming he opened his eyes once more and found that it was really true. His black-and-white checked cap, which he had carefully placed last night, as usual, on the floor beside his bed, actually was drifting gently under the table like a tug passing under Waterloo Bridge.

Albert sat up, pushed back the blankets and put his feet on the floor, then he lifted them again suddenly with a yelp. The floor was awash with two inches of cold water. Carefully he stood up and tucked the bed clothes out of the way, then he paddled over, collected his cap which was gently butting against the leg of his chair and hung it over the tap to drip into the sink. While he was there he filled the kettle and put it on.

After he had lit the gas ring, Albert sloshed through the water to the window and looked out. The rain was falling in torrents and as he watched there came another flash of lightning and a great crash of thunder overhead. There was a little waterfall running down the steps and several inches of water in the area which must be seeping under the door. There was nothing Albert could do just then, so he reached up to the peg for his black-white-

and-blue checked Sunday cap, placed it firmly on his head, and looked round at the damage. Actually, not much harm had been done except to his cap and the hearthrug which he rolled up and placed firmly against the door. Then he made himself a pot of tea.

27

Albert was just spreading honey on a second slice of bread when he realised the rain had stopped and the sky was brighter. Then he heard a very exciting noise: a siren which rose and fell and got louder and louder. A fire engine!

Splashing over to the window he opened it and looked out just in time to see a big red engine stop right outside, and then a pair of black boots came down the steps. A big, tall fireman in a black helmet called out to him, "Are you all right in there?"

"I'm fine, thank you, sir," answered Albert.

"Much water in there?"

"About two inches, I think."

"Don't worry, we'll have you pumped out in no time," and the boots clumped up to the street, to return in a moment trailing a great big hose-pipe.

Albert was terribly excited. He was not quite sure what being pumped out meant, but it sounded very interesting. The hose was laid in the area. There was a loud sucking noise and the level of water began to go down. When the area was empty, Albert opened his door and the big fireman brought the hose in and soon all the water was slooshed back up to the street and down the drain.

"You'll have some mopping up to do," said the fireman.

"That's all right," Albert replied, "I'll soon get that done. You've been very kind. Would you care for a cup of tea?"

"I'll have to make it a quick one, but I won't say no. Got some more flooded basements to pump out. What's your name?" he asked as he gulped his tea down quickly.

"Albert."

"Well, Albert, how would you like to come and ride

on the engine and watch us working?"

"Me!" gulped Albert.

"Yes, come on!" and the big black boots clumped up the steps again followed by a speechless bear in his best Sunday cap. For the next hour or two Albert was in

Heaven. He sat up in the seat beside the driver and away they went further up the street to the next flood area.

Being very careful not to get under their feet, Albert managed to be right there on the spot to watch the busy firemen, up and down the steps, pumping out the water and helping people to rescue their belongings. Albert did what he could, and once, when an old lady was being helped into a taxi and sent off to stay with her daughter until her home had dried out, Albert carried her canary in its cage out to the taxi and then ran back to rescue her little portable radio before it got wet.

When all the pumping was finished and the firemen had done all they could to help, they said Albert must come back to the Fire Station for a visit, and off they all went with Albert up in the front of the great red engine.

At the station the men took off their big helmets and changed their wet clothes. They showed Albert the room above the station where they waited to be called to a fire or a flood, or sometimes to rescue someone from a roof with their long ladder. They had even been called to get a cat out of a tree. Most exciting of all to Albert was the big brass pole through a hole in the floor of the room above the garage down which the men could slide quickly and on to their engines. Albert wanted to try, but it was quite a wide pole and the first time he went down much too fast and landed sitting down with his cap over one eye, but he plodded up the stairs and tried again and soon he could slide down easily and land on his feet, and then he made the firemen laugh by climbing back up the pole.

When they were all dry again they took Albert along to the canteen with them and gave him a big plate of steak and kidney pudding, followed by a lovely sticky

piece of treacle tart.

He was just licking the last of the treacle off his paws, when there was a terrific clanging noise and the men leapt up, grabbed their helmets and slid, one after another, down the pole and on to their engines.

"It's a fire this time," Albert's special friend called to him. "Sorry we can't take you with us, but you might get hurt. Come and see us again," he shouted over his shoulder.

Albert slid down the pole for the last time just in time to wave and call "Thank you and goodbye," as the great engines shot out of the garage and up the street, their sirens wailing.

He stood a little forlornly watching them disappear and then, full of dinner, with his best Sunday cap firmly on his head, he started for home and the job of mopping up his lino.

That night, for once, his dreams did not take him on to the deck of his sailing ship, but behind the wheel of a great red monster racing down the road with a big black helmet on his head, ready to fight a fire with the help of his gallant men.

IV

ALBERT LENDS A PAW

There were two things Albert was very fond of—the docks and chips.

Sometimes he would give himself a very pleasant afternoon by combining the two and taking a bag of chips, sprinkled with salt and vinegar, down to the docks where he would perch on a bollard, eating his chips and watching the dockers unloading the big ships. The men on the ship would load boxes on to a big net and then the edges were pulled together and fixed on to the hook of the crane. At a shout, Bill, the crane driver, in his little cab high above the dock, would pull a lever and the great load would lift out of the hold of the ship and land gently on the ground. Then the boxes were loaded on to lorries or packed into warehouses.

One day Albert was happily finishing the last few crispy chips (he always left the crisp bits till last) as he watched a ship come in and tie up. She was hardly still, and the gangway down, before the dockers were swarming over her, lifting the hatches and preparing to unload.

Bill was swinging the crane over ready for them when the foreman, George, came over and said, "Hello there, Albert, how would you like to lend a hand. I'm short of men today and I have no one to check in."

"Who? Me?" Albert couldn't believe his ears.

"You can write, I suppose?" asked George.

c

"Of course I can write," Albert answered indignantly, "although not very well," he added in case he was taking on something too difficult for him.

"Oh, you'll only have to make ticks on this paper." George had a sheet of paper fixed on a board on which he was busy writing as he spoke. "I want you to sit by the doorway into the warehouse and make one tick for every box carried in. Could you do that?"

"Of course I can, and I'd like very much to help." Albert got down off his perch and followed George.

"What are they unloading?" he asked.

"Australian honey," George remarked over his shoulder. Albert stopped in mid-step. Then he slowly put his foot down and whispered huskily, "Honey?"

"Yes, Australian honey, Orange Blossom, Clover, several kinds."

Albert cleared his throat. "Australian honey. Made by Australian bees, I suppose?"

"Yes, of course." George suddenly realised Albert wasn't following him and turned back to see him gazing at the ship, murmuring to himself, "Tons and tons of honey. A whole SHIPload of honey!"

George laughed. "I suppose all bears are pretty fond of honey."

Albert dragged himself away and went on slowly towards the warehouse. "Yes," he answered, "I think you could say all bears are pretty fond of honey."

All afternoon Albert sat on his box making a tick for every box carried into the warehouse, taking only a break for a cup of tea with the men. Sometimes there would be a short wait for the next load and Albert would gaze at the piles and piles of boxes in the warehouse and picture to himself all those hundreds and hundreds of jars of beautiful golden, sticky, sugary, deLISHus honey.

By six o'clock all the unloading was finished and the warehouse closed. George collected the clipboard from Albert and told him to come along to the office with him.

35

Once inside the office, George said, "It's not easy to pay you wages for your help because you're not regularly employed here, so I hope you will accept this present from us."

"That's all right," answered Albert, "I enjoyed . . ."

His voice died away as he saw his present. George had found a shallow box and packed into it two dozen small jars of honey in neat rows. There were six jars each of Orange Blossom, White Clover, Pale Honey Gold, and a very special one called Extra Rich.

Albert recovered his voice enough to say that it was the most wonderful present he had ever had, and soon afterwards he and his precious box were given a lift by a lorry taking dock-workers home.

Soon the kettle was on the gas ring, the table was laid, and in the middle of the cloth the flames of a bright little fire were reflected in the deep, dark gold of a jar of Extra Rich honey.

V

ALBERT GOES ON PARADE

It was Easter Monday morning and Albert was in Petticoat Lane. He had been in bed with a bad cold for a few days and Mrs Cooper, who lived in the top part of 14 Spoonbasher's Row, had very kindly been looking after him. She had brought him bowls of nice nourishing soup and hot lemon drinks with a spoonful of his own honey in them. She wanted to rub his chest with camphorated oil, but Albert had objected to this because he would have such a job washing it out of his fur.

Now he was better and had stopped coughing and sneezing, so he had come out shopping with his blue string bag. One of the things he was going to buy was a bunch of daffodils for Mrs Cooper, to say thank you.

His friend, Mrs Arbuthnot, picked him out a very nice bunch, still in bud, so that they would last, and wrapped them in green tissue paper.

Albert was on his way home with his shopping bag full of bread and butter, half a pound of sausages and a packet of tea, when he noticed a stall selling Easter eggs. He went over and stood looking at the different eggs; big ones with pink and yellow sugar flowers on them, eggs filled with chocolates and standing in pretty boxes and smaller ones in silver paper.

Suddenly Albert thought of his friend Henry, and he decided to take him an Easter egg as a surprise. Albert

picked out a small egg wrapped in silver paper and tied
with a blue bow. He paid for it and carefully carried it
home.

After putting his shopping away, he took the daffodils
up to the front door of the house and gave them to Mrs
Cooper who said, "Thank you very much, Albert, but
you shouldn't have bothered," and Albert said, "You
were very kind to me," and they had a little chat about

what a lovely spring day it was and that Albert must be careful of his chest even if it was sunny.

Because Mrs Cooper thought the wind might be a bit treacherous, Albert pulled his cap down to his ears a bit more firmly and wrapped his bright red muffler round his neck before he set off for the junk-yard carrying Henry's egg.

When he reached the big gates in Candle Lane he found them open and wandered in. He saw Henry in his stable and went over. Henry's owner, Mr Higgins, was busy brushing Henry's back with a big brush, and Albert saw that Henry was looking very smart and shiny, and that the cart, standing in the yard had been newly painted bright yellow, picked out in red, and decorated with paper roses.

"Good morning, Henry. Good morning, Mr Higgins. Are you going somewhere special?"

"We're going in the Easter Monday Parade through Hyde Park," Mr Higgins told him.

"I do look rather smart, don't I?" remarked Henry. "Am I going to wear my brasses?"

"Oh, blimey!" grumbled Mr Higgins, "that means half an hour's polishing."

"What are your brasses?" asked Albert.

"There they are, on the wall."

Hanging from two nails was a broad leather strap from which dangled six round brass medallions about four inches wide, each one a different design.

"I could polish them for you," Albert offered. "I

always clean the knobs on my bed and my fender."

"Good for you," said Mr Higgins. "You'll find the things in that box in the corner."

"This is very decent of you," said Henry as Albert sat down on an old chair and began to rub on metal polish.

"I know it's silly, but I always rather fancy myself in my brasses."

By the time the grooming was finished and Henry's harness, newly polished, was in place, the medallions were shining and Albert helped Mr Higgins fasten the strap across Henry's chest, where they sparkled in the sun and jingled cheerfully with every movement.

"Now you look very smart," Albert said as he stood back to admire.

"Do I really?" Henry looked a little bashful.

"Well after all that work you'd better ride in the parade with us," Mr Higgins suggested.

"Could I?" gasped Albert.

"There's plenty of room up on the seat beside me. Now run off home and smarten yourself up. I shall be ready to start in half an hour."

Albert turned to leave when Henry called to him, "Have you forgotten your parcel?" and he remembered.

"I brought you an Easter egg," he told Henry as he opened the cardboard box, "But I forgot all about it when I saw you." And he held out the egg.

"Thank you very much," said Henry and closed his mouth over the egg.

"Wait a minute," Albert snatched it away again. "Let me take off the ribbon and silver paper. You're not supposed to eat those."

"Well, you didn't say," explained Henry, "and I've never had an Easter egg."

Albert undid the ribbon and peeled off the paper, then he held out the chocolate which Henry munched in his big teeth.

"We could tie the ribbon in his mane," said Mr Higgins, and he carefully tied the blue bow between Henry's ears.

"Now you hurry along and get ready."

Albert ran all the way home and put on the kettle. While it heated he took down his Sunday cap and brushed it hard. On the table was a little bunch of primroses Mrs Cooper had brought to cheer him up. He searched in the cupboard for a pin and fastened the flowers to his cap. He used the hot water to scrub his face and paws and then he carefully combed his fur till it was all lying in the right direction, put on his cap and trotted back to Candle Lane.

He reached the yard where Henry stood between the shafts of the bright yellow cart just as Mr Higgins came out of his door. At the sight of him Albert's mouth fell open.

Mr Higgins was wearing a black suit and on it were sewn hundreds and hundreds of pearl buttons. There were rows of small ones round the sleeves and circles and whirls of all sizes from tiny ones to buttons the size of a penny all over the jacket. His cap had circles of buttons all round the crown, and you couldn't see the brim for twinkling pearl.

"You're a Pearly," gasped Albert.

Henry looked round and laughed at Albert's astonishment. "Looks all right, doesn't he?" he asked. "You'll see the King and Queen of Pearlies this afternoon, I expect."

Mr Higgins climbed up on to the seat and pulled Albert up beside him. In a bracket on the side of the cart was a long whip with a big red bow tied round it.

Mr Higgins took it out and gave it a loud crack over Henry's head.

"Watch it," said Henry, and he pulled the cart out of the gate and into the street.

Before long they reached the Serpentine in Hyde Park and joined up with dozens of other trade carts, all gaily

decorated and driven by people in top hats, red coats, pearly suits and all sorts of smart clothes. They were given places in the procession led by a wonderful brass band, and the whole lot moved off down Rotten Row between crowds of people. All the women were wearing bright spring dresses and new Easter bonnets.

The Pearly King and Queen were riding on a big red cart behind two great grey horses. You couldn't see their clothes for twinkling buttons, and a great plume of feathers tossed above the Queen's hat.

Behind them came the little yellow cart pulled by Henry, his head held high and his brasses jingling and shining across his broad chest.

Beside Mr Higgins, bolt upright, the long whip clutched in one paw, yellow primroses bobbing cheerfully on his Sunday cap, sat the proudest, happiest bear in the whole, wide world.

VI

ALBERT IS INVITED TO TEA

The sun was warm on the back of Albert's neck as he leaned over the stern of the barge, trailing his paw in the cool, green water.

He was on a pleasure cruise through London and, earlier, while they were waiting for a few more passengers, Bill, the owner, had sat beside Albert in the sunshine and told him all about the barges.

"There are not very many about these days," Bill had said, "and most of those have motors but, a few years ago, there were hundreds of barges carrying goods through the miles of canals in England. The families lived on board and the children went to school on odd days wherever they happened to be.

"They were always decorated the same way," he went on, pointing to the panels on the side of the little cabin, "castles and roses, always castles and roses, and they kept the cabins spotlessly clean, with lots of polished copper pans and jugs always shining brightly, like those down there," and he pointed to two water cans standing on a shelf winking gaily.

"On the other side of the cabin you can see a row of horse brasses that they used to hang on the horses which pulled the barges."

"I know about horse brasses," said Albert, "because my friend Henry wears them when he goes anywhere special. The horses walked along the towpaths, didn't they?" he asked.

"That's right, but they couldn't go under the bridges, so the barge people had to get through by pushing their feet against the walls of the tunnels."

Now they were drifting gently under tall grey houses and the motor was making soft chugging noises.

"This is where the artists live," Bill told his passengers and Albert was very interested to see a man sitting on a stool in front of an easel, painting busily at a large canvas.

"I think he's painting us," he said.

"Well, he'll have to hurry up, because we won't wait, we're going down Regent's Park canal, through the Zoo."

Soon they could hear roaring and howling and shrieks and squawks and the houses were left behind for green banks and trees through which they could see glimpses of cages and people strolling about.

"Look," said one of the men, "there is a lion on top of that hut!" Everyone turned to look. "And there's a tiger in that tree and a big snake hiding under that bush!"

They realised that he was pulling their legs and Bill said, "Yes and there is a hippo in the water."

Albert looked at the piece of driftwood and said, "That's not a hippo, that's a crocodile!"

They all laughed and stood looking round them as the boat chugged lazily along the still water.

Suddenly the man said again, "Look, there's a monkey loose."

Nobody took any notice and he said again, "No, I'm not joking, there is a large monkey on the bank."

"You're right," replied Bill, "I think it is a chim-panzee. It must have escaped."

"Shouldn't we try to catch it?" asked Albert.

"They are quite fierce," said Bill, "they have a very nasty bite." He thought about it and then said, "Still I suppose YOU would be quite safe, I shouldn't think a monkey would eat a Teddy Bear!" He seemed rather amused at the idea and Albert felt a little huffy about it.

"If you would please pull into the bank, I'll see what I can do," he announced with dignity.

The barge turned into the bank and Albert jumped out on to the grass and walked over to the chimpanzee.

The animal seemed about to run away, but it changed its mind and came up to Albert and took him firmly by the paw.

"I think he likes you," called Bill. "Here comes one of the keepers," he added.

A keeper came running along the path and looked very relieved to see Albert with the chimpanzee.

"Lulu, you bad girl," he grumbled, "what do you mean by running away? Thank you very much for catching her," he added, turning to Albert. "They were just going into the big cage for their tea party, when she slipped away," and he held out his hand to take the chimp's paw, but she said "Whoo whoo" and clung tightly on to Albert.

"Could you possibly walk as far as her cage with her and then she might go in without any trouble?" asked the keeper.

"I don't mind," asnwered Albert, "but I'm on a cruise with that barge and I can't keep them waiting."

Bill joined them at that moment and heard what Albert said.

"Why don't you stay with your new friend?" he suggested, "and you can have your trip all over again with me tomorrow."

"Could I really? I'd like to stay, I've never seen the chimps' Tea Party."

So the barge chugged off down the canal with Albert and Lulu waving to it and Lulu calling "Whoo whoo".

The keeper led the way back up the path and they came to the big open-air cage where all the other chimpanzees were sitting round a table. They all got very excited when they saw Lulu coming back, clinging tightly to Albert.

At the door of the cage she still would not let go of him, but dragged him in and up to the table.

"You'd better stay to tea," laughed the keeper, so Albert sat down at the table and the keeper poured him out a mug of tea from a huge pot and Lulu gave him her own bun.

Word soon went round the Zoo about the strange new guest at the Tea Party and soon an even bigger crowd than usual was peering in at them.

Albert was enjoying himself. He didn't mind in the least being stared at, and he thought the chimpanzees delightful, with good table manners.

51

"This is a very nice cup of tea," he remarked, as he borrowed Lulu's spoon to scoop up the lovely sticky mess in the bottom of the mug, six large spoonfuls of sugar.

When it was time for the chimps to go back to their home again, Albert walked round with them and Lulu went quite happily with the others, but she waved and called "Whoo whoo" rather sadly as she watched Albert leave.

"You must come and see her again," the keeper told him, "and now I am going to take you round the Zoo and show you the other animals. I expect they will be interested to meet you, come to think of it."

Albert had a wonderful time. The lions did some very fierce roaring for him and he tried to growl back at them, but his keeper friend said he didn't really sound very ferocious.

The tigers stalked proudly backwards and forwards across their cages, rubbing themselves against the bars and ignoring Albert, but it was the seals he liked best.

He was fascinated to watch them catching their herrings as they dived through the air into the water, making hardly a splash. The keeper told him that seals could be trained to balance a ball on their nose and all kinds of clever tricks.

Albert found all the different bears very friendly. In fact, he was still chatting to the panda when the keeper told him that it was closing time and asked if he would like to be tucked up in a spare cage for the night.

Albert knew he was only joking, but he hurriedly said that it was quite time he was going home and thank you for a very pleasant afternoon. The keeper said again that they were very grateful to him for his help with Lulu and that he really must come and see her again, whenever he liked.

Riding home in the bus, Albert thought over his day and how much he had enjoyed himself. "And I am going for my barge trip again tomorrow," he told himself and he began to wonder if he might buy some paints and an easel and if it would be difficult to clean the paint off his fur afterwards.

VII

ALBERT PLAYS THE DUKE

The letter plopped on the mat just as Albert was finishing his breakfast.

He read it through and then he read it again with growing excitement. His cousin Angus was arriving that very day to watch the football match that afternoon between England and Scotland.

The letter had taken several days to reach him and there was only about an hour before Angus would be there!

Albert dashed about tidying up and making his bed, then he grabbed his shopping bag and his leather purse from behind Grandfather's clock and hurried down to the shops.

"What's all the hurry?" asked the grocer, putting a packet of ginger nuts into a paper bag.

"My cousin Angus is arriving soon to see the match," Albert told him. "He has two tickets and he is going to take me with him. They say the Duke is going to kick off and I have never seen him."

"You are very lucky," said the grocer. "It is very difficult to get tickets for a big match. I wish I could go." Then he went on, "I tell you what, shall I lend you my rattle?"

"Your rattle?" asked Albert, puzzled and thinking of babies.

"My big rattle that I take to the matches. You whirl it round and round and it makes a lovely noise."

"Oh yes, I know what you mean. Yes, please, I would love to borrow that."

Mr Henderson went through the door to the room at the back, where he lived and came back with a great big rattle, which was painted in red and blue stripes.

55

"That's beautiful! Thank you very much. I promise to take great care of it."

Albert packed his parcels into his bag and turned to go.

"Wait a minute," called Mr Henderson, "take these for your cousin," and he gave Albert a packet of Scotch oatcakes. "He will enjoy these with some of that special honey of yours, if you have any left."

"What a good idea. Yes, I have three pots left and I was going to have one of them for tea. Thanks again."

Albert had reached home and put away his shopping when there was a knock at the door. He hurried to open it and there stood Angus. He was a little taller than Albert and he was wearing a small tam o'shanter hat and a bright red tartan muffler.

"Angus, how wonderful to see you and what a big surprise. I only got your letter an hour ago."

"The post must be very slow down here," remarked Angus. "How are you Albert? You are looking very well, but I think you are fatter!"

"It is probably all the honey I have been eating lately," replied Albert. "Sit down by the fire and get warm while I make you a cup of tea."

He put the kettle on the gas and poked up a nice cheerful blaze. Angus settled down in the big basket chair and Albert pulled a wooden one up beside him.

They had a good hot cup of tea and Albert told Angus how he had been given all the honey and Angus told Albert how he had been given the tickets for the match by an uncle who wasn't able to go at the last minute.

"I came down on the special train they run and I shall be going back on it tonight."

"Well, we'll have an early lunch and then I will give you a good tea before you go."

Albert had brought in some fish and chips for lunch, because he thought he would like to give his cousin from Scotland something very English, but Angus told him they often had it at home, and it was really his favourite food, but Albert was not to tell Aunt Bertha that, because she would think that he ought to like haggis best.

The two bears had a good gossip about all they had been doing and ate their fish and chips in front of the fire out of the paper, as they both agreed that this was the way they tasted best and then Albert said it was time they set off for the football ground.

They went by tube train because Angus had never seen one. He was a little bit scared and hung on to Albert as they went down the moving staircase, but, by the time they reached their station, he had quite recovered and wanted to go up and down the escalator again, but there wasn't time and Albert promised they would go home the same way.

They arrived at the ground and found their seats, which they were very pleased to see were right at the front and beside the passage where the players came out!

The two of them looked happily round and Angus said he thought the only better seats in the whole place would be in the directors' box!

Just as they sat down a band came marching out on to the pitch and began to play music for community singing. Albert and Angus sang as loudly as anyone and thoroughly enjoyed it, especially when they played "Loch Lomond".

When it was time for the kick-off, it was very exciting to watch the two teams running out from just beside them and forming up into two lines facing each other on the pitch. There they stood and nothing happened!

After a few minutes, as the players began to look at each other, a man came out and spoke to the two captains and the crowd watched as the three men looked round them and then the captain of the English team pointed and it seemed as if he were pointing straight at Albert! He was! The third man suddenly left the other two and came over to Albert and said, "Excuse me, I am the manager of the English team. The Duke has sent a message to say that he is held up by a traffic block and he wants us to carry on without him. Would you care to kick off for us?"

Albert's mouth fell open. No words would come.

Then he felt Angus nudging him and saying, "Of course he will kick off for you. He'll be very glad to— won't you, Albert?" Now Angus was pushing him out of his seat and into the gangway. "And I'll come with him," he added.

And Albert was out on the pitch, with his mouth still open and Angus by his side, chatting happily with the manager.

Albert managed to close his mouth again while he was introduced to the Scottish team and Angus was introduced to the English team, but it was not until he was set in front of the ball that he gasped out, "I've never kicked a ball!"

"Never mind," answered the manager, "all we need is for you to get the ball into play."

Albert went back a few paces and ran forward, kicking the ball so well that everybody gasped with amazement, except Albert, who was flat on his back and could not see where the ball had gone.

With a wild, highland whoop, Angus was off after the ball, but the manager, who had introduced himself as Mr Calder, grabbed him and pointed out that now they must get out of the way of the players. Angus was disappointed, but he helped heave the still dazed Albert to his feet and they ran to the side of the pitch.

"Now," said Mr Calder, "it's only right that you should both come and sit in the directors' box."

This time it was Angus who was flabbergasted, but he soon recovered, and the two bears followed Mr Calder up the steps and into the comfortable chairs of the big open box.

Two minutes later, all three of them were yelling their heads off and Albert was madly waving his rattle encouraging their own teams to score.

At half-time there had been no score and everyone enjoyed the drinks that were passed round to ease throats hoarse with shouting.

Suddenly the manager prodded Angus and Albert and said, "Here he is, at last."

"Who?"

"The Duke."

"Here!"

"Of course. Come and be introduced."

Clutching checked cap and tam o'shanter, they were introduced to the Duke who actually *thanked* them for helping him.

"Not at all, we were very pleased to do it," Albert managed to gasp out.

Although he was shouting and waving his rattle for the English team, Albert was secretly rather pleased when the Scottish team won by two goals to one. After

saying a very contented goodbye and thank you all round, the two bears went home by the tube train again, but Angus was too full of the match to want to do any extra riding on the moving stair.

Albert stirred up the fire and put on some coal and

then he prepared a big tea, for they were very hungry. It was while they were buttering their second oatcake and Albert was passing the last pot of Extra Rich honey that Angus said, "Why don't you come up to Stirling next week for the Highland Games?"

"Could I?"

"Yes, of course. You'd like it very much. Caber tossing and putting the shot and wrestling and all the Scottish dancing. Will you come?"

"I certainly will. It is quite a while since I had a holiday, and I haven't seen Aunt Bertha for such a long time."

They talked of the things they would do together in Scotland and then it was time to leave for the station. King's Cross was packed with happy, shouting Scots going home after winning the match. Angus found a seat and Albert stayed with him until the long train pulled out of the great station and he waved till it was out of sight.

As he went contentedly home, Albert thought about his coming visit to Stirling. "I might buy myself a kilt," he said.